MR. JELLY
and his Small Friend

Roger Hargreaves

MR. MEN   **LITTLE MISS**

MR.MEN™ LITTLE MISS™ © THOIP (a Sanrio company)

Mr Jelly and his Small Friend © 2014 THOIP (a Sanrio company)
Printed and published under licence from Price Stern Sloan, Inc., Los Angeles.
First published in France 1998 by Hachette Livre
This edition published in 2015 by Dean, an imprint of Egmont UK Limited,
The Yellow Building, 1 Nicholas Road, London W11 4AN

ISBN 978 0 6035 7124 4
61260/1
Printed in Great Britain

EGMONT

Mr Jelly was frightened of everything.

In fact, he was terribly, terribly frightened of everything.

The slightest sound would send him running to hide under his bed, shaking and trembling just like a jelly.

Poor Mr Jelly!

Knock! Knock!

The terrible sound frightened Mr Jelly out of his wits.

And again.

Knock! Knock!

Quivering with fear, Mr Jelly started opening all the bolts and locks on his door.

It took him quite a while! And all the time he muttered to himself, "Oh my goodness me. Whoever could it be? Robbers? Thieves? Oh calamity!"

Finally he opened the last lock and there on his doorstep stood Little Miss Tiny.

"Hello, Mr Jelly," she began. "I was just passing and I thought you might like to come with me into the forest to collect strawberries."

"The forest?" exclaimed Mr Jelly. "Oh goodness me, no! Who knows what we could find. Snakes? Bears? Lions? Oh calamity! But after your walk do come back to have lunch with me."

So off she went, alone.

It was long after lunchtime and Mr Jelly was starting to get very worried indeed.

Perhaps Little Miss Tiny was lost in the forest.

What could he do? What should he do?

Mr Jelly gathered together all his courage, and shaking and trembling he stepped out of his house and into the forest to look for his little friend.

"Little Miss T … T … T … Tiny!" he called, his teeth chattering with fear.

The only reply was the wind in the trees.

Scared out of his wits, Mr Jelly ran all the way back to his house …

… and grabbed the telephone.

"Hello, Mr Rush?" he said. "I n … n … need your help to find Little Miss T … T … Tiny. I'm afraid she is lost in the forest. She could have fallen into the river, or she could have been eaten by wolves or dragons! Oh calamity!"

One minute later, Mr Rush arrived at Mr Jelly's house.

Another minute later, Mr Rush left and disappeared into the forest running at full speed.

"Little Miss Tiny, where are you?" he called. "I don't have any time to lose. I'm in a terrible hurry!"

But, not finding her, he rushed away again.

Sometime later, Little Miss Contrary called on Mr Jelly. She had heard that Little Miss Tiny was missing.

"Goodbye!" said Little Miss Contrary. "I've come to not help."

Mr Jelly was rather frightened and very confused but he let her in.

Little Miss Contrary opened the wardrobe door and looked through the piles of sheets and towels.

"Ah! Just as I thought," she said. "Little Miss Tiny isn't there. Hello!"

And off she went.

"How strange," thought Mr Jelly, shaking all over.

Now night was falling and large, black clouds were gathering in the sky. It looked like a big storm was coming.

Again, gathering together all his courage, Mr Jelly ventured back to the edge of the forest.

There he met Mr Bounce.

"You're my last h … h … hope," stammered Mr Jelly. "You must help me find Little Miss T … T … Tiny before it's too … too … too late!" And he hurried back to his house as fast as his shaking legs would carry him.

BOING!

BOING!

BOING!

Mr Bounce bounced higher and higher looking for Little Miss Tiny. But no matter how high he bounced he couldn't see her.

Suddenly the sky was lit up with lightning and Mr Jelly's house shook to the sound of thunder.

He couldn't leave Little Miss Tiny all alone in the storm.

So, shaking with fright at each clap of thunder, he threw himself out into the dark, stormy night.

"Help! Help!" came a voice from the forest.

Do you think it was Little Miss Tiny? No, not at all. It was Mr Jelly, who had seen a worm!

At the sound of his shouts, Little Miss Tiny came running to help.

"Mr Jelly!" she exclaimed. "What on earth are you doing out in the forest in a storm? You must be scared out of your wits. Let me take you home. And I'll tell you all about the lovely day I've had."

Back at Mr Jelly's house they were celebrating with a large strawberry cake, covered in cream, when …

BOING!

SPLAT!

Mr Bounce bounced right into the house and landed on top of the cake!

"Oh calamity!" shouted Mr Jelly. "What will become of us? The sun has fallen from the sky!"

And with another, rather sticky SPLAT …

... he fainted!